"*Happy Birthday, Ruby* is a gentle introduction for families to openly talk about their son or daughter that died. It is a beautiful celebration of a little life that gives all grieving families permission to do the same and a delightful insight into ways a family can celebrate and honour their child together."

Amanda Bowles, President
Bears Of Hope Pregnancy & Infant Loss Support Inc.
www.bearsofhope.org.au

Published by Tate Publishing & Enterprises, LLC
127 E. Trade Center Terrace | Mustang, Oklahoma 73064 USA
1.888.361.9473 | www.tatepublishing.com

Tate Publishing is committed to excellence in the publishing industry. The company reflects the philosophy established by the founders, based on Psalm 68:11,
"The Lord gave the word and great was the company of those who published it."

Book design copyright © 2011 by Tate Publishing, LLC. All rights reserved.
Cover and interior design by Chris Webb
Illustrations by Kurt Jones

Published in the United States of America
ISBN: 978-1-61346-258-4
Juvenile Fiction / Social Issues / Death & Dying
11.08.02

Happy Birthday, Ruby

Tate Publishing & Enterprises

written by KATHRYN DALLA FONTANA

In memory of Jacob Samuel Poile,
an angel who was born sleeping.

Dedicated to Madeleine,
for remembering, loving, and living.

As the sun peeps through my curtain, I know that, at last, the day has arrived. "Hip hip hooray." I leap out of bed. "Today is Ruby's birthday."

Ruby is our sister. She would be three today, but she died just before she came out of Mum's tummy. She doesn't live with us. She lives in heaven with the angels. Even though Ruby doesn't live in our house, she is part of our family. We think and talk about her every day. Today is special because we celebrate her birthday.

I dash into Ruby's garden. It is a quiet corner of our backyard where an angel sits, listening to the wind chimes tinkle and gazing at butterflies who flutter by. I pick some forget-me-nots. We planted these on the day Ruby went to heaven.

I run inside to give the flowers to Mum. Mum puts the forget-me-nots in the vase on Ruby's memory table, where carved wooden angels sit and watch over us.

"Happy birthday, my angel," I hear Mum whisper to herself.

We huddle on the lounge as Dad opens Ruby's keepsake box. It is a box filled with all of the special memories from when Ruby was born. It has her teddy bear and the quilt that the hospital gave us to bring home, the candle from her blessing, ink prints of her tiny little hands and feet, photos of Ruby, wrapped in her blanket, with Mum and Dad, and even a lock of her hair. Dad finds a poem that he wrote on the day that Ruby went to heaven. He reads it to us. A tear rolls down Mum's cheek.

This year, tucked under the box on Dad's lap, is a present for Mum. The card says, "May I be in your heart forever." Mum opens the present. It is a necklace holding a heart-shaped pendant, with Ruby's name engraved across the centre. Mum has the biggest smile on her face as she puts on the necklace. "Always," she says out loud. "Always."

I am busy making a birthday card for Ruby. This year it is the shape of a butterfly, painted with glitter and decorated with sequins and photos of us celebrating Ruby's birthday last year. I think that it is beautiful. I'm sure Ruby will too.

We go to Ruby's resting place. I put her card and birthday present, a tea set and new pair of fairy wings, next to the plaque with her name on it. I tell Ruby the fairy wings are a spare just in case her angel wings get dirty and need a wash. Mum and Dad give each other a big hug and say nothing.

Dad gives each of us a balloon. We each write our own message. Mine says, "Happy birthday, Ruby. Hope the angels like your chocolate tea. Big hugs and kisses. Chloe." We take the tags off and let the balloons float up to heaven so that Ruby can play with them. Heaven really is a long way away.

Back at home, we prepare for our party. We are all busy. Mum is making party food and a birthday cake. Dad is trying hard to blow up balloons. His cheeks are red, and he is puffed. Matt sets the table with party hats, poppers, and hooters.

This year, our new baby brother, Jack, is at our birthday table. I tell him all about Ruby. He is too little to understand yet. One day, he will know that Ruby is his special sister in heaven.

We sing "Happy Birthday" and each take turns blowing out the three candles on Ruby's cake. We hug in a circle and sing our family song.

Big or small, near or far
I love you for who you are
You are very special to me
You are part of my family

Looking out the window, I see the stars. Tonight, they are brighter than ever. Mum smiles. She knows what I am thinking.

"That is Ruby smiling at us. She is happy too," Mum says.

I look back at the stars. "Happy birthday, Ruby. I love you."

About the Author

Kathryn Dalla Fontana lives in Sydney, Australia, with her husband and two young children. Since beginning her own family, Kathryn's life now revolves around children, especially her own. *Happy Birthday, Ruby*, Kathryn's first book, was inspired by a chat with her friend's six-year-old daughter, whose brother had died and now lives in heaven with the angels.

e|LIVE

listen|imagine|view|experience

AUDIO BOOK DOWNLOAD INCLUDED WITH THIS BOOK!

In your hands you hold a complete digital entertainment package. In addition to the paper version, you receive a free download of the audio version of this book. Simply use the code listed below when visiting our website. Once downloaded to your computer, you can listen to the book through your computer's speakers, burn it to an audio CD or save the file to your portable music device (such as Apple's popular iPod) and listen on the go!

How to get your free audio book digital download:

1. Visit www.tatepublishing.com and click on the e|LIVE logo on the home page.
2. Enter the following coupon code:
   69ea-4378-1c84-60b1-1049-1b63-ab05-8d5e
3. Download the audio book from your e|LIVE digital locker and begin enjoying your new digital entertainment package today!

Lightning Source UK Ltd.
Milton Keynes UK
UKOW07f1146261114

241977UK00016B/122/P